This Book Belongs To:

_____

Values To Live By™ Classic Stories

Alice in Wonderland

Black Beauty

Call of the Wild

The Jungle Book

Pinocchio

Robinson Crusoe

Secret Garden

Swiss Family Robinson

Treasure Island

20,000 Leagues Under the Sea

Wonderful Wizard of Oz

VALUES TO LIVE BY™

www.valuestoliveby.com

ISBN 0-9747133-2-5
ISBN 978-0-9747133-2-8

FREDERIC THOMAS INC.
Produced by: Frederic Thomas Inc., Naples, Florida, Tel: 239-593-8000.

A Classic Story About Honesty
Pinocchio

By Carlo Collodi
Retold by Margo Lundell
Illustrated by Isidre Mones

Managing Art Editor Tom Gawle
Senior Editor Mary Weber
Designer Tim Carls

FREDERIC THOMAS INC.

Pinocchio

Pinocchio may well be the most famous puppet in history. His story was first published in 1881 as a weekly series of adventures in an Italian magazine for children. The series was an astounding success. Children across Italy could hardly wait for each week's new episode. By 1883, the series was sold as a children's book by an Italian publisher. Over the next 20 years, the story was translated and published in many countries in Europe, North America, Asia and Africa.

Since Pinocchio's story first appeared, it has been turned into plays, puppet shows, a ballet and opera and 17 motion picture films.

The story of Pinocchio *has been translated and published in many countries.*

Visitors in the Villa Garzonni, in the village of Collodi, Italy stand in the mouth of the whale, one of the many sculptures found in the gardens, celebrating the story.

Carlo Lorenzini, the author of *Pinocchio*, used the pen name of Carlo Collodi. Collodi was actually the name of the beautiful medieval village in Tuscany, Italy, where the author's mother had grown up. The author himself was raised in the city of Florence, but he often visited the nearby town of Collodi as a child and may have imagined it as the setting for Pinocchio's story. In Collodi today, there is a commemorative park (above) to visit, built to celebrate the famous little puppet.

VALUABLE FOOTSTEPS

Stories like *Pinocchio* are fun to read and think about, but can also teach us about the world and ourselves. *Pinocchio* is a great story to teach us about the word *honesty*. Being honest means that you are trustworthy and people can believe what you tell them. You can learn more about the value *honesty* by trying to understand what the story characters may be thinking or feeling and how they view the world.

Try the following little activity with a parent, sister, brother or friend while you read the story. First, watch for footsteps within the book pages. They will lead you to a special paragraph where you can pretend to be one of the story characters. By "walking in his or her shoes," you can begin to understand that character. Then talk about how you would feel and what you would do if you took that character's place. Would you feel pleased, or would you be angry? What could you do to help someone do what is right? Why do you think it is important to be honest?

Many years ago, in a small town in Italy, there lived a carpenter named Gepetto. Gepetto was a lively old man who had little money, but was content in his work. Still, Gepetto was lonely. At long last he came up with an idea. He would make a wooden puppet, and the puppet would keep him company.

Gepetto found especially fine, hard wood to make a puppet boy. He was pleased with his plan and began carving as soon as he could.

"I shall call my puppet Pinocchio," he said. "The name will make people smile and will bring him luck."

The carving went well, but odd things began to happen as Gepetto worked. When he finished Pinocchio's mouth, the puppet laughed at him. After he made Pinocchio's two little wooden feet, the puppet gave him a kick. "Oh dear," said Gepetto. "You are barely finished Pinocchio, and you are already behaving like a bad boy. What have I done?"

What happened next was even more troubling. As soon as Gepetto taught Pinocchio to walk, the naughty puppet ran out the door and into the street. Gepetto ran after him, shouting, "Stop, Pinocchio! Stop!" Passers-by were amazed when they saw the old man chasing a puppet. Finally, a policeman grabbed Pinocchio by his rather long nose and brought him to a halt. When Gepetto caught up to them, he took hold of Pinocchio and shook him.

"You will be punished for this!" he shouted. "Wait until we get home." When the crowd that had gathered heard Gepetto's angry words, they felt sorry for Pinocchio. They were afraid that Gepetto was going to break the little puppet in two. Gepetto was so mad and the crowd was so upset about the whole business that the policeman ended up setting Pinocchio free and taking Gepetto off to jail.

"I did nothing wrong!" cried Gepetto, as he was dragged away. "I only tried to make a wonderful puppet." Gepetto was sobbing as they neared the jail.

As for Pinocchio, he ran off happily, heading straight back to Gepetto's house.

The policeman took Gepetto off to jail.

Pinocchio reached home and settled comfortably into Gepetto's favorite chair. Suddenly he heard a strange sound. *"Cri-kit! Cri-kit!"*

Pinocchio looked around and saw a big cricket on the hearth by the fireplace. "Who are you?" he asked.

"I'm the Talking Cricket," said the large insect. "I've lived in this room for many, many years."

"Go away," said Pinocchio impatiently. "This is my room now!"

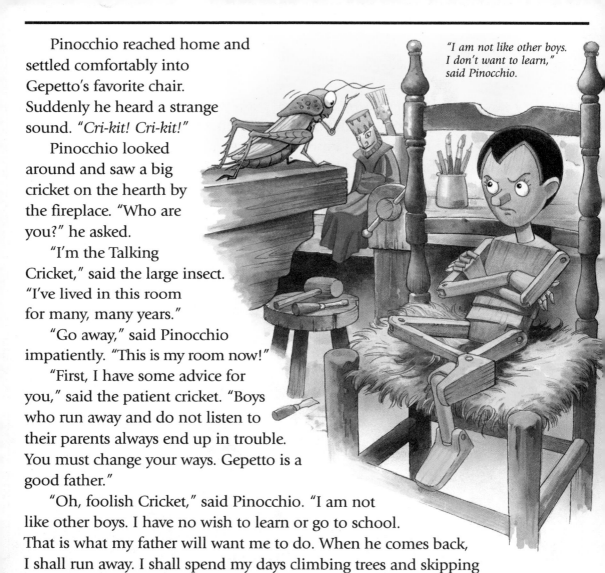

"I am not like other boys. I don't want to learn," said Pinocchio.

"First, I have some advice for you," said the patient cricket. "Boys who run away and do not listen to their parents always end up in trouble. You must change your ways. Gepetto is a good father."

"Oh, foolish Cricket," said Pinocchio. "I am not like other boys. I have no wish to learn or go to school. That is what my father will want me to do. When he comes back, I shall run away. I shall spend my days climbing trees and skipping stones on the river."

The cricket and Pinocchio began to argue, and it ended badly. Pinocchio picked up a hammer from Gepetto's work table and threw it at the cricket. It knocked the cricket across the room and out of sight. After that, Pinocchio realized he was very hungry. His stomach cried out for something to eat, but there was no food in the house. Evening came and Pinocchio grew tired in spite of his hunger. He finally fell asleep.

Pinocchio promised never to run away again.

When Gepetto came home the next morning, he brought bread and milk with him for breakfast. He had no money for anything more. When Pinocchio saw his father carrying the food, he clung to him and said, "Papa, I'm so hungry. You must feed me. I am sorry that I ran away. I will not do it again. I will even go to school if you say that I must."

Gepetto sighed. "Boys always make promises when they want something," he said.

"But I am telling the truth," said Pinocchio. "I will go to school and study hard."

Gepetto looked at Pinocchio severely and said nothing.

"Papa, I am so hungry," Pinocchio cried. He began to sob. He hung his little wooden head and hugged his stomach.

Gepetto was a man with a big heart, and he could not stand to see Pinocchio in such a sorry state. Quickly, he put breakfast on the table. As the two ate, Gepetto told Pinocchio how glad he was that the puppet would be going to school. He said he would make Pinocchio a suit of clothes after breakfast.

"I will start tomorrow," said Pinocchio, reaching for another piece of bread. "I will."

The next morning, Pinocchio started out for school, skipping down the road. "I will learn to read today," he said to himself. "Tomorrow I will learn to write. I will be a fine student."

Pinocchio's grand thoughts were interrupted by the sound of a band marching down the street. *"Boom, barra boom!"* banged the drum. *"Toot, turra toot!"* sang the horns.

"Oh dear," Pinocchio said to himself. "I promised my papa I would go to school today. But the music is so merry, I must follow along."

A small crowd trailed through the town after the band. It led them to a big, brightly painted puppet theatre. Inside the theatre, a show was just beginning. Pinocchio could not help himself. He had to see the show. He slipped into the theatre and found himself a seat. Two funny puppets named Harlequin and Punchinello were onstage arguing with each other and making everyone laugh.

Pinocchio couldn't believe his eyes. The actors on the stage were wooden puppets, just like himself. In his excitement, Pinocchio suddenly jumped onstage. Then he performed a dozen handsprings. He stole Harlequin's hat and threw it to Punchinello. The three puppet boys made up a silly skit as they went along, and the audience loved it.

After the show, the director asked Pinocchio to stay and be a regular member of the cast. Pinocchio knew he should go home to Gepetto, but being in the show was fun. He finally agreed to stay. He would live at the theatre with the other actors. ✎

Pinocchio Meets a Fox and a Cat

After many days and many shows at the theatre, Pinocchio decided he had to go home. He had kept his father waiting too long. He said good-bye to Harlequin, Punchinello and the others and he started back to Gepetto's house. He knew Gepetto would be upset after his long absence, but Pinocchio planned to give his father the five gold coins he had earned at the theatre. "The money will help Papa," he said to himself.

As he walked, Pinocchio happened to meet two travelers, a fox limping on one lame foot and a cat who appeared to be blind. Pinocchio said a friendly good morning to them. The Fox whispered to the Cat, and the Cat nodded in agreement.

"Hold on, young sir," said the Fox. "Would you be interested in hearing a secret that will make you rich? If you have a little money, we know how to multiply it many times over."

"You do?" Pinocchio answered. "I have money that I am taking home to my father." Pinocchio pulled out his gold coins to show the Fox. At the sight of the money, the Fox jumped up and down on the leg that was supposedly lame. The blind Cat's eyes widened, as if she had perhaps seen the money.

Pinocchio showed Fox and Cat the coins.

After he saw Pinocchio's coins, the Fox seemed to force himself to speak calmly. "Young man," he said, "We can be of help to you. Here is what you must do to increase your money. We will take you to a town called Simple Simon. Outside of town is an extraordinary field called the Field of Miracles. There you will bury your money. Then, if you pour two pails of water on the spot and wait until the next morning, a tree will grow that is heavy with gold coins."

Pinocchio was determined to return to Gepetto. He wondered if the poor man had not been worried by his absence. But Pinocchio was very interested in what the Fox was saying. "Oh my!" he said excitedly. "How many coins will there be on the tree?"

The Fox shrugged. "Oh, a thousand, two thousand," he answered.

"Can it be true? How wonderful!" cried Pinocchio forgetting then and there about his papa. "Let us be off at once."

Pinocchio dreamed of the money tree.

The Fox and the Cat linked arms and headed off with Pinocchio in the direction of the Field of Miracles. They walked and they walked, until much of the day was gone. Finally, the Fox and Cat announced they were too hungry to go any further. They begged to stop at an inn along the way. Pinocchio wanted to get to the Field of Miracles as soon as possible, but he agreed to the delay. When they came to the inn, the three went in and ordered a meal.

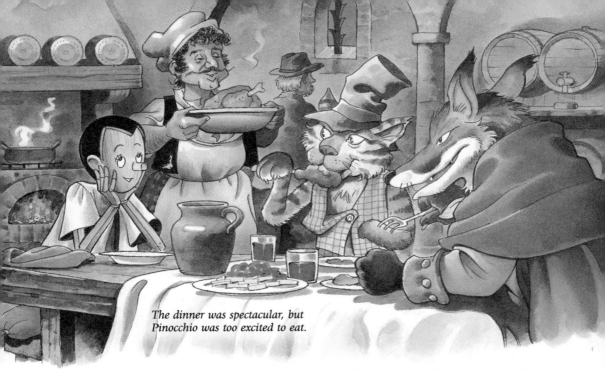

*The dinner was spectacular, but
Pinocchio was too excited to eat.*

The dinner was spectacular. Pinocchio was still too excited to eat, but the Fox and the Cat ate enough for six. The Fox gulped down several platters of chicken croquettes. The Cat consumed a mountain of delicately sauteed sardines and shrimp. After the meal, the Fox and the Cat were so sleepy they wanted to spend the night at the inn. Pinocchio could not change their minds and let the innkeeper lead them to small upstairs bedrooms. The innkeeper promised to wake them early in the morning.

Long before the sun came up the next morning, the innkeeper banged on Pinocchio's door. "Wake up, sir!" he shouted.

"Are my companions ready?" asked Pinocchio.

"Your friends have already departed," the innkeeper answered. "They said they had an important errand to do. They left directions to the place where you are going. They will meet you there."

The innkeeper slipped the directions under the door along with a bill to be paid. Pinocchio dressed quickly. Before he left the inn, he was obliged to give the innkeeper money for food and lodging for three. Then he started down the dark road by himself. ✎

The thieves chased
Pinocchio across the fields.

Just then, two figures covered in burlap sacks ran out of the shadows.

"Give us your money!" they cried, as they fell upon Pinocchio. They knocked the puppet down. Suddenly, they heard the clink of coins in Pinocchio's pocket. Somehow the puppet got up and began to run. Quickly, he reached for the coins and put them into his mouth. If the thieves caught up to him, they would not find the money.

Pinocchio ran and ran, across fields and through vineyards. The thieves were never far behind. Finally, Pinocchio came to a small white house. He knocked at the door with all his strength. A window opened and a beautiful woman with pale blue hair looked out. Just as she went to open the door, the thieves caught up to Pinocchio and pulled him back by the collar. They dragged him from the house to a nearby wood. They searched his pockets, but could not find his coins. Angry, they hung him by his coat from the branch of a tree called the Big Oak.

"We will be back tomorrow," said one thief. "Then you will tell us where you have hidden your coins." After that the thieves disappeared into the dark, leaving Pinocchio dazed and bruised, hanging from a tree limb.

The Blue Fairy

Pinocchio was soon rescued by the beautiful woman with blue hair who lived in the house nearby. She was in fact a Blue Fairy and she knew Pinocchio's life was in danger. She sent a falcon, a particularly large, strong bird, to pluck the puppet from the Big Oak and fly him to her.

The Blue Fairy discovered that Pinocchio was ill with a high fever and quickly put him to bed. Then she mixed some medicine in a glass. The Blue Fairy held it out to Pinocchio, but the puppet refused to drink.

"I am sure it is bitter," he said, making a face.

"It is bitter, but it will do you good. I will give you a lump of sugar after you swallow it," said the Blue Fairy gently.

"But I want the sugar now," Pinocchio insisted.

The Blue Fairy gave in and let him have the sugar, but Pinocchio still would not drink what he called the "bad bitter water." In fact, it took much more coaxing on the part of the Blue Fairy before Pinocchio would take the medicine. Then, a few minutes after he swallowed it, he jumped out of bed feeling quite well. That is because wooden puppets who take medicine from a Blue Fairy recover very quickly.

The Blue Fairy tried to give Pinocchio his medicine.

When Pinocchio was feeling himself again, the Blue Fairy asked him to explain how he ended up hanging from a tree branch. Pinocchio told her the story of his dear father and the showman who had given him gold pieces and the thieves who had attacked him in the night. The Blue Fairy listened with great interest, for she was already very fond of Pinocchio.

"And the gold coins," she said. "Where have you put them?"

"I lost them," Pinocchio answered, even though the coins were in his pocket. No sooner had he told a lie than his nose suddenly grew several inches longer.

"And where did you lose the coins?" the Blue Fairy asked.

"In the wood near your house."

At this second lie Pinocchio's nose grew longer still. After he lied a third time, his nose grew so long he could not move it in any direction without hitting a wall. The ridiculous nose made the Blue Fairy laugh. She knew it had grown because of the lies Pinocchio told. To teach him a lesson, she let Pinocchio moan and cry for half an hour. Then she called in a dozen woodpeckers. The birds perched on the nose and began to peck. Wood chips flew, and soon the nose was back to its usual size. Pinocchio was very grateful.

As soon as he told a lie, Pinocchio's nose grew several inches.

Pinocchio thought his troubles were over at last. The Blue Fairy had invited him to live with her, and she sent word to Gepetto to come and live at her house as well. Pinocchio was overjoyed and set out to meet his father on the road.

Unfortunately, before he had gone very far he met the Fox and the Cat. They greeted each other in a very friendly manner. Soon the Fox and the Cat were busy telling Pinocchio that he could still go with them to the Field of Miracles. Again, Pinocchio was tempted by the thought of 2,000 gold coins. He forgot all about his promise to the Blue Fairy to return home soon.

It was a long walk. Finally, they reached the Field of Miracles, which looked like any other field. Pinocchio dug a hole and quickly buried his coins. Then he filled his shoes with water, since he had no pail, and watered the hole.

This time the Fox told Pinocchio he would only have to wait one hour for the tree full of coins to grow. The threesome went into a nearby town to wait, but soon the Fox and the Cat announced they had to leave on another important errand.

"We wish you luck, Pinocchio!" said the Fox as they parted.

When Pinocchio returned to the Field of Miracles by himself, his heart was beating fast, but he found no tree. He dug up the hole where he had buried the coins, but he found no money at all. The puppet sat down and wept.

At last, Pinocchio gathered himself up and set out on the high road that led back to the Blue Fairy's house. He realized that the Fox and Cat had tricked him and stolen his coins. "I have been so foolish!" he said over and over. "From now on, I will do better."

He reached the top of a hill near the Blue Fairy's house. He could see the woods where he had hung from the Big Oak, but there was no white house in the field nearby. Pinocchio was broken-hearted.

"Dear Blue Fairy!" he cried. "Where are you?"

At that moment a large pigeon swooped down to the ground next to him. "I think you must be Pinocchio," he said politely.

The puppet was very surprised, but the Pigeon went on to explain that he had been looking for Pinocchio. He knew Pinocchio's father. He said Gepetto had been searching everywhere for his son and had finally built a boat. The desperate father planned to sail the seven seas to look for Pinocchio.

The Pigeon flew with Pinocchio to the shore where Gepetto had built his boat.

Pinocchio asked the Pigeon to fly him to the stretch of shore where Gepetto was launching his boat. The Pigeon agreed, and off they flew, with Pinocchio sitting on the big bird's back. When they arrived at the shore at last, Gepetto was already far out at sea. A storm had come up, and the little boat was sinking. Pinocchio watched helplessly from the shore.

"Pigeon, what will happen to my father?" he cried.

"There is a huge fish in these waters called the Dog Fish," said the Pigeon. "I am afraid it will swallow your father up."

Pinocchio said good-bye to the Pigeon and turned away sadly from the seashore. He had nowhere to go. He walked this way and that, thinking about the father who was lost to him. Finally, Pinocchio realized he was hungry. He began to beg for food from those passing by, but no one would help him. Some asked him to work for the food he wanted, but Pinocchio was still too proud to work.

At last a woman came by carrying two pails of water. She wore a shawl over her hair. By then Pinocchio was faint with thirst and begged the woman for water. The woman asked him first to carry the two pails to her house. There she would give him water and a meal as well. Pinocchio set his pride aside at last and carried the water to her house.

When they reached the house, the woman took off her shawl. It was then that Pinocchio saw her blue hair.

"Can it be?" he asked. "Are you my good fairy? You are! I have missed you so, and I have suffered so. Please forgive me." The puppet began to sob.

The Blue Fairy agreed to help Pinocchio become a real boy.

When he was calmer, Pinocchio and the Blue Fairy talked and talked. Pinocchio told her of the mistakes he had made and how tired he was of being a foolish puppet. He longed to be a real boy instead.

The Blue Fairy smiled and agreed to help Pinocchio become a boy. All he had to do was tell the truth, go to school and do what the Blue Fairy asked him to do. Of course, Pinocchio agreed.

Soon Pinocchio was in school. You can imagine how the children laughed when they saw a puppet walk into the class! Pinocchio paid no attention to their teasing and showed himself to be a friendly fellow and a good student. Everyone grew to like the puppet and wanted to be his friend.

Actually, Pinocchio was too friendly. He trusted everyone, even boys in school who were not trustworthy. The Blue Fairy knew about these friendships and warned Pinocchio that some of the boys could lead him into trouble.

"No fear of that!" Pinocchio would answer.

For one year Pinocchio studied hard and did everything the Blue Fairy asked of him. At the end of the year he passed his exams at the top of his class. The Blue Fairy was pleased and called Pinocchio to her.

"Now I can grant your wish, Pinocchio," she said. "Tomorrow you will no longer be a puppet. You will be a boy instead, and we will have a party to celebrate. You may go and invite all your friends."

Pinocchio clapped his hands. How happy he was! He hugged the Blue Fairy as hard as he could. Then he ran off to invite his friends to the party. He ran from house to house, passing out invitations. Everyone agreed to come. Finally there was only one more friend to find, a boy named Candlewick.

Candlewick was not the boy's real name. It was a nickname because the boy was as thin and tall as the wick of a new candle. In truth, Candlewick was a lazy fellow who did not always do his schoolwork, but he was one of Pinocchio's very best friends.

It was late when Pinocchio found Candlewick. The boy was standing at the corner of a dark lane. Pinocchio tried to invite his friend to the party, but Candlewick had other plans. "I have to wait here until midnight," he whispered, although there was no one to hear. "Then I am going away."

"But where are you going?"

"To a country called the Land of Play. It is the best place in the world for boys. There is no school there, and every day is a holiday. Oh, it is a wonderful place. You just have fun from morning to night. It is the place for me. A coach will come by soon to pick me up. Pinocchio, why don't you come, too?"

Pinocchio shook his head. He said he must be getting back to the Blue Fairy's house, but he stayed to hear more. As Candlewick went on talking, Pinocchio began to forget his promise to the Blue Fairy. He forgot about the party and becoming a boy. All he could think about was not having to study anymore and the fun he would have with Candlewick. Then they heard clattering on the cobblestones, and a coach drove into view.

The coach to the Land of Play drove into view.

The Land of Play

Pinocchio hesitated a long time, but finally he decided to go with Candlewick to the Land of Play. There was no room in the carriage because it was already full of boys, but Pinocchio and his friend were able to ride two of the donkeys pulling the carriage.

The donkeys pulled the coach through the night. As he rode, Pinocchio thought it was odd that donkeys were hitched to the coach instead of horses, but he said nothing. It was stranger still that the donkeys, instead of having plain hooves like regular donkeys, wore boots made of white leather. Once or twice in the night Pinocchio thought he heard one of the donkeys crying. He paid no attention.

In the morning, they arrived in the Land of Play. What a remarkable place. In the town square, boys were riding bicycles, rolling hoops or splashing in the fountain. Others were chasing each other or playing ball. Acrobatic boys were walking on their hands with their feet in the air.

On the walls of the houses there were chalk messages, such as "Down with School!" and "Free Forever!" Boys came rushing up to the coach to welcome the newcomers and lead them to the houses where they would live. As the boys led Pinocchio away, they whooped and hollered to each other until you almost had to cover your ears. What noise! What happiness!

Life was such a pleasure in the Land of Play that weeks and months passed by in a flash. Pinocchio could not believe his good fortune. One day when he and Candlewick were sitting in the square eating chocolate eclairs, Candlewick reminded Pinocchio of the old days.

"Just think," he said. "You were going to go home to the Blue Fairy that last night and miss all of this. I talked you into coming. That means I am a good friend."

"You are indeed," Pinocchio answered. "I have been really happy for these five months, and I owe everything to you."

As Pinocchio sat with Candlewick, he rubbed his ears because they were bothering him. That night he went to bed, not knowing that he would soon have very different ears.

During the night his ears changed into the long, furry ears of a donkey. The next morning, the puppet stared in the mirror.

"I should never have run away!" he cried, pulling at his hateful new ears. "I never should have come to this place."

Pinocchio hurried to find Candlewick. Lo and behold, Candlewick had donkey ears, too. As the two friends stood and cried together, they felt their faces and bodies change. Little by little they were covered with gray fur and felt the urge to bray.

Before the day was over, Pinocchio understood that the Land of Play was a successful business run by villains. The owners of the business lured boys to the Land of Play, then waited until they behaved like, and turned into, donkeys. Finally, the donkeys were sold to the highest bidders. Soon, Pinocchio was sold to a circus owner. At the circus he was forced to jump through so many hoops that he became lame in one leg. The circus owner then sold him to a man who wanted a donkey for nothing more than his leather hide.

Pinocchio was led along a cliff by the sea, heading for his life's end. Suddenly, the puppet knew he had been on these cliffs before. It was the very place he had stood and watched his father's boat sink in a storm. Pinocchio decided he must try to escape. He pulled away from his owner. Then he jumped off the cliff into the sea below.

As Pinocchio the donkey sank into the sea, an enormous school of fish swam up and surrounded him. The fish were sent by the Blue Fairy, who had not forgotten Pinocchio and knew now that he was in trouble. The fish nibbled and nibbled at Pinocchio until there was no more donkey to be seen. Pinocchio was a puppet once again. He quickly bobbed to the top of the water.

"Thank you, Blue Fairy," he whispered as he began to swim. "I know you are the one who is helping me, even though I don't deserve it."

Pinocchio found that he was a good swimmer. This made sense since he was made of wood. However, before the puppet had swum a hundred yards, a sea monster rose out of the water. It was the enormous Dog Fish, the creature who had swallowed Pinocchio's father.

Suddenly, tumbling head over heels, Pinocchio was washed into the mouth of the terrible fish. He landed in the creature's gigantic stomach. When he came to his senses, there was darkness all around. There seemed to be a tiny speck of light in the distance, and Pinocchio went to take a closer look. What he saw made his heart leap up. It was an old man seated at a table, eating a plate of fish by candlelight. The old man looked like Pinocchio's father. ✎

A sea monster named Dog Fish rose out of the water!

Pinocchio and Gepetto Are Reunited

Pinocchio and the man eating fish stared at each other.

"Papa! Is it you?" Pinocchio asked, his heart beating quickly.

"Yes, Pinocchio! Yes!" his father answered.

Pinocchio wanted to laugh and cry and say 1,000 things at once. Instead, he threw his arms around his father. When they could speak, Pinocchio's father began telling his son how his boat had been swallowed by the Dog Fish during the storm that Pinocchio had witnessed. Gepetto said he had lived for months on the food he had stored away in his boat.

Then it was Pinocchio's turn to tell his father about his many misfortunes. He told Gepetto, too, how sorry he was that he had ever run away. "I will never leave you again, Papa," said Pinocchio, and he knew this time he was telling the truth.

Pinocchio then talked to his father about trying to escape from the Dog Fish's stomach. "We will find our way back to the mouth of this fish, jump into the sea and swim away."

Gepetto did not believe it was possible because he was a poor swimmer. Pinocchio told his father he, himself, was an excellent swimmer, and all would be well.

Pinocchio was right. He and his father made it to shore. They dried themselves on the beach and then went in search of food and lodging. Soon they came to a simple house with a tile roof. Pinocchio knocked on the door and heard a voice say, "Come in." They went inside and looked around. There was no one to be seen.

"I am here!" someone said. "This is my house." Pinocchio looked and saw a large cricket sitting on the hearth. It was the Talking Cricket, the very one Pinocchio had thrown a hammer at long ago. Pinocchio told the cricket how sorry he was for his past deed. Then he explained the sad state he and his father were in. He asked for bread and water and a place for his father to rest.

"I will have pity on you both, father and son," said Cricket, "but I want you to remember the cruel treatment I received. It may teach you that in this world, when it is possible, we should show courtesy to everybody if we wish to have it extended to us in our time of need." He forgave Pinocchio and told him he and his father could stay as long as they wanted, provided Pinocchio was prepared to

"This is my house," said the Talking Cricket.

work for his keep. In the days that followed, Pinocchio went out and found work on a neighbor's farm. Soon he was earning enough to pay the cricket for food and lodging for his father and himself. He worked long hours and did not complain.

Pinocchio and his father spent five good months at the Talking Cricket's house. One night, Pinocchio had a dream about the Blue Fairy. He dreamt that she came and kissed him on the forehead and said, "Well done, my Pinocchio. You have shown a good heart – and a good head to go with it. You will be rewarded." ✎

A Boy at Last

When Pinocchio awoke the next morning, he yawned and stretched out his arms. Then he saw they were not the arms of a puppet. He ran to the mirror. What he saw looking back at him was a boy, a boy like other boys, a bright-looking boy with chestnut hair. Pinocchio thought he was dreaming.

He was even more amazed when he looked around the room. He was no longer in the Talking Cricket's house. He was in Gepetto's old home instead, freshly painted and filled with handsome furniture. In a daze, Pinocchio went to find his father.

In his workroom, Gepetto was sitting in his favorite old chair, for that chair still remained. He smiled when he saw Pinocchio.

"Papa, look!" said Pinocchio, kneeling by his father. "I am a boy, a regular boy. How could this happen?"

"You have told me about the Blue Fairy," Gepetto answered. "Might this be her doing? Or perhaps you have earned the right to be a boy."

Pinocchio did not understand what had happened or if he would ever see the kind Blue Fairy again. What he did know was that his most hoped-for wish had come true. Pinocchio was a boy at last. ✎

What do you think?

Reading a book is like taking a magic carpet ride into a new and different world. While in Pinocchio's fairy tale world you experienced exciting adventures right along with the little wooden puppet! Classic stories like this one are fun to read, but also teach us about the world and ourselves. Wouldn't it be fun to share what you've learned with a brother, sister, friend or parent? Find a quiet place to talk, then use the questions on the next two pages to discuss *Pinocchio* and the valuable lessons it teaches.

1. *Honest* people are trustworthy – you can believe what they say. What's the best way to make sure that people trust you?

_____

_____

_____

_____

_____

_____

2. Gepetto said, "Boys always make promises when they want something." Is it honest for boys or girls to make promises that they do not plan to keep?

_____

_____

_____

_____

_____

3. Pinocchio often did what troublemakers told him to do. What would you do if someone like Candlewick tried to get you to do something that you knew was wrong?

_____

_____

_____

_____

_____

_____

_____

4. What made Pinocchio change his ways and become a good boy?

_____

_____

_____

_____

_____